This Faber book belongs to

....

....

To all of you out there who dream of flying. (Never say never!) — J.C.
For my beloved husband and son — E.S.

PRAISE FOR HARRY & LIL

'If this gem of a book is anything to go by, there is a partnership to rival Donaldson and Scheffler.' Books for Keeps

'Whimsical and enticing.' Metro

'A lovely, beautifully illustrated book, perfect for family snuggles. We really liked all the animals, especially the owl.' Mischa and Asher, ages 4 and 2

'A Julia Donaldson-style rhyming text that works brilliantly for young children . . . A lovely book. Don't miss it!' Serendipity Reviews

'The perfect picture book.' Armadillo Magazine

'I like Candy Stripe Lil because she never gets frightened.' Bella, age 3

'A perfect combination of clever rhymes and beautiful illustrations.' Sunday Express

'Take a smidgeon of *The Gruffalo*, a tiny pinch of *Foggy Foggy Forest* and some truly charming artwork, and you're half way towards imagining how great *Hog in the Fog* is.' Read it Daddy

First published in the UK by Faber and Faber Limited
Bloomsbury House, 74–77 Great Russell Street, London WC1B 3DA

Text copyright © Julia Copus, 2016
Illustration copyright © Eunyoung Seo, 2016

Printed in China

HB ISBN 978–0–571–32529–0
PB ISBN 978–0–571–32530–6

10 9 8 7 6 5 4 3 2 1

The moral rights of Julia Copus and Eunyoung Seo have been asserted.
A CIP record for this book is available from the British Library.

➤ A FABER PICTURE BOOK ◄

A
Harry
& Lil
Story

The Shrew that Flew

Julia Copus

Illustrated by
Eunyoung Seo

ff

FABER & FABER

One Saturday, in the middle of June,
on a bright and windy afternoon,
all the creatures by Piggyback Wood
were getting ready – as fast as they could.

There was only a short time left to prepare
for the birthday party at Badger's lair.
At the top of the invitation it said:
Will guests please arrive with a hat on their head.

Will guests please arrive
with a hat on their head.
Birthday Party
2:15pm
Badger's Lair
please come!

Of all the creatures on Piggyback Hill,
busiest of all was Candy Stripe Lil.
"Oh dear," she sighed. "There's so much to do,
and the party begins at a quarter past two."

Harry had polished his tusks and hooves
and even the grooves between the hooves.
On his head was the most spectacular hat —
part spotty, part dotty, part pointy, part flat!

Lil's hat was hanging to dry on the line.
"It's a good job," she said, "that the weather is fine."

The washing went flip; the washing went flap.
Then – in front of their eyes – Lil's favourite cap
worked itself loose from where it was pinned
and was tugged away by a gust of wind!

Over the bench and the garden hose,
up, up and away it rose —

till it snagged on the edge of a chimney slate.
"Oh no!" cried Lil. "Now we're going to be late!"

"Good grief!" Harry said, peering up at the sky.
"You'd have to fly to get up that high."
"You're right," said Lil. " . . . So that's what we'll do!
If birds fly, why can't shrews fly too?"

"Because," Harry said, "shrews don't have wings."
"Maybe not," said Lil, "but I've other things.
I'm sure we'll find something to help me to fly.
There's all sorts of stuff in the shed we could try."

In the depths of the shed was a shopping trolley,
an old lawnmower, a folded-up brolly . . .

"Look!" squeaked Lil. "That's just what we need!
With the help of this brolly we're bound to succeed."
Lil opened the brolly over her head.
"Hold on! There's a gust on its way," Harry said.

Lil gripped very tight; the umbrella bent
and **trembled**,
then **tugged**,
then – **whoosh!** – up she went!
and floated off – past the sycamore stump . . .

. . . then landed again, on a large moss clump.
She landed so quickly she let out a yelp.
"Oh dear!" Harry cried, rushing over to help.

"It will never work. Your hat's lost forever."
"Nonsense!" said Lil. "You should never say never!"

Back in the shed was a rusty old wheel,
a bucket, some bunting, a shoe with no heel,
a hand-me-down blanket from Candy Stripe Gran,
a wellington boot, a portable fan . . .

"Look!" squealed Lil. "That's just what we need!
With the help of this fan, I *know* we'll succeed."

Lil fastened the fan to the top of her head.
"Hold tight! There's a gust on its way," Harry said.

The blades began whirring, then – wheeesh! – off she took.
She went up so high that she hardly dared look.

But when the wind dropped, she fell, with a bump,
and landed again on the same mossy clump.

"Oh dear!" Harry cried, "I don't like this at all.
The more you go up, the further you fall.
We'll never succeed. Your hat's lost forever."

"What nonsense!" said Lil.
"You should never say never!"

It was then that a sound came: tac, tac, tac.

"I know that sound," said Harry to Lil . . .
It was Deer! On his way down Piggyback Hill.

"A fine day," Deer said. "Will you walk with me?
I'm just off to Badger's birthday tea."

Tied to his antlers, by a golden thread, was a **GIANT** balloon, in a shimmering red.

Harry pointed a buffed and gleaming hoof
to where Lil's cap lay, trapped on the roof.

"You'll never reach it," said Deer. "Not ever."

But Harry and Lil cried . . .
"NEVER SAY NEVER!"

They pulled the balloon down low to the ground.
Lil took the string and, without a sound,
she tied one end to Harry's tail.

"Last chance," she whispered.
"We mustn't fail."

Harry lined up his tail with the chimney pot,
and when Lil let go — up she went. Like a shot!

She reached for the hat — it was there in her grasp —
when, beneath her, the others let out a gasp:
a strong breeze had wrenched it out of her paws . . .

. . . and she *just* grabbed it back,
by the tips of her claws!

"She's done it!" cried Harry. "Amazing!" said Deer;
"Let's hear it for Lil!" – and he let out a cheer.

Lil tied the hat firmly on to her head.
"If we hurry, we'll just make the party," she said.

When Lil and her friends at last appeared
all the animals clapped and cheered!

They queued long
into the afternoon
for a go on the magical
flying balloon.

One after another they stepped up to try
but *they* were all too heavy to fly.

The only creature
who managed that
was Candy Stripe Lil –
in her favourite hat.